VALENTINE'S DAY SURPRISE

By Robin Wasserman
Illustrated by Duendes del Sur

ABDOPUBLISHING.COM

Reinforced library bound edition published in 2017 by Spotlight, a division of ABDO. PO Box 398166, Minneapolis, Minnesota 55439. Spotlight produces high-quality reinforced library bound editions for schools and libraries. Published by agreement with Warner Bros. Entertainment Inc.

Printed in the United States of America, North Mankato, Minnesota.
042016   092016

THIS BOOK CONTAINS
RECYCLED MATERIALS

PUBLISHER'S CATALOGING IN PUBLICATION DATA

Names: Wasserman, Robin, author. | Duendes del Sur, illustrator.
Title: Scooby-Doo and the Valentine's Day surprise / by Robin Wasserman ; illustrated by Duendes del Sur.
Description: Minneapolis, MN : Spotlight, [2017] | Series: Scooby-Doo early reading adventures
Summary: Scooby and the gang are excited for Valentine's Day. But all of their valentines are missing! Did a ghost take their valentines or does Scooby have a secret admirer? It's a case only Scooby can solve.
Identifiers: LCCN 2016930655 | ISBN 9781614794745 (lib. bdg.)
Subjects: LCSH: Scooby-Doo (Fictitious character)--Juvenile fiction. | Dogs--Juvenile fiction. | Valentine's Day--Juvenile fiction. | Valentines--Juvenile fiction. | Ghosts--Juvenile fiction. | Mystery and detective stories--Juvenile fiction. | Adventure and adventurers--Juvenile fiction.
Classification: DDC [Fic]--dc23
LC record available at http://lccn.loc.gov/2016930655

Spotlight
A Division of ABDO
abdopublishing.com

Scooby and the gang were excited to celebrate Valentine's Day.

They sent valentines to all their friends and family.

They couldn't wait to receive valentines in the mail too.

But when they opened the mailbox, they were sad to find it empty.

"Do you know where our mail is?" Velma asked the mailman. The mailman was very confused. He scratched his head and thought for a minute. "I'm not sure," he said. "I'll have to retrace my steps."

"We'll help you," said Fred.

"Let's search for clues!"

But Scooby and Shaggy were scared.

"Like, what if a ghost took our valentines?" asked Shaggy.

"Rhost!" said Scooby.

Scooby jumped into a bush to hide.

"Come on, Scooby," Velma said.

"We need your help to find our valentines."

Scooby shook his head and the bush shook too.

Then he thought he smelled Scooby-Snacks.

Scooby came out of the bush to look for the Scooby-Snacks.

"We should ask the mailman to help us," said Velma.

The mailman drove Scooby
and the gang to Mrs. Feldman's
house.

"I dropped off a lot of valentines
at this house," said the
mailman. "Then I was chased
down the street by a dog."

"Do you remember what the
dog looked like?" asked Daphne.

"She was wearing a red bow,"
said the mailman.

Everyone looked for clues in
Mrs. Feldman's yard.
Scooby found something
yummy.
Velma picked up something
small and red.
"Is it a bow?" asked Daphne.
"It's an empty candy wrapper,"
said Velma.
"I feel like we're getting closer,"
said Fred.

Scooby sniffed around the yard.
He followed a trail of empty
candy wrappers across the street
to Mr. Peterson's fence.
At the fence he found more
candy and he ate it!

Scooby jumped over the fence to Mr. Peterson's house.

He couldn't believe what he found.

There was Mr. Peterson's dog, Rosie...

Rosie had their valentines and all their candy!

The gang had all received valentines from their friends and family.

Shaggy got a box of chocolates from his cousin Jennifer.

Fred and Daphne received flowers and a card from their friend Julia.

Velma got a stuffed teddy bear from her aunt Susan.

But Scooby only got a card... where were his Scooby-Snacks?

Scooby searched through Rosie's
pile of cards.

He found lots of cards and
chocolates.

But he did not find the
Scooby-Snacks.

Rosie poked her head around
the tree and watched him.

Then she barked to get Scooby's
attention.

Scooby turned around and
saw Rosie holding out a box of
Scooby-Snacks just for him!
It was Scooby's best Valentine's
Day ever!
"Scooby-Dooby-Doo!" barked
Scooby.

The End